This book belongs to

_____

Ganesha
Ravana and the Magic Stone

Script
Sourav Dutta

Illustration, Lettering and Design
Rajesh Nagulakonda

Editing
Jason Quinn

Desktop Publishing
Bhavnath Chaudhary

Mission Statement

To entertain and educate young minds by creating unique illustrated books
that recount stories of human values, arouse curiosity in the world around us,
and inspire with tales of great deeds of unforgettable people.

Published by Kalyani Navyug Media Pvt Ltd
101 C, Shiv House, Hari Nagar Ashram,
New Delhi 110014, India
ISBN: 978-93-81182-24-6

Printed in India

Ganesha

Ravana and the Magic Stone

Sourav Dutta   Rajesh Nagulakonda

CAMPFIRE®

KALYANI NAVYUG MEDIA PVT LTD

Ganesha

Shiva
Father

Ravana
King of Lanka

Narada Muni
Traveling Brahmin

The King of Lanka, Ravana his name,
in search of glory, in search of fame,
look how thrilled he is as he sets forth,
to the faraway lands of the north,
to collect for himself a magic reward
that Shiva had promised him, or so he heard.

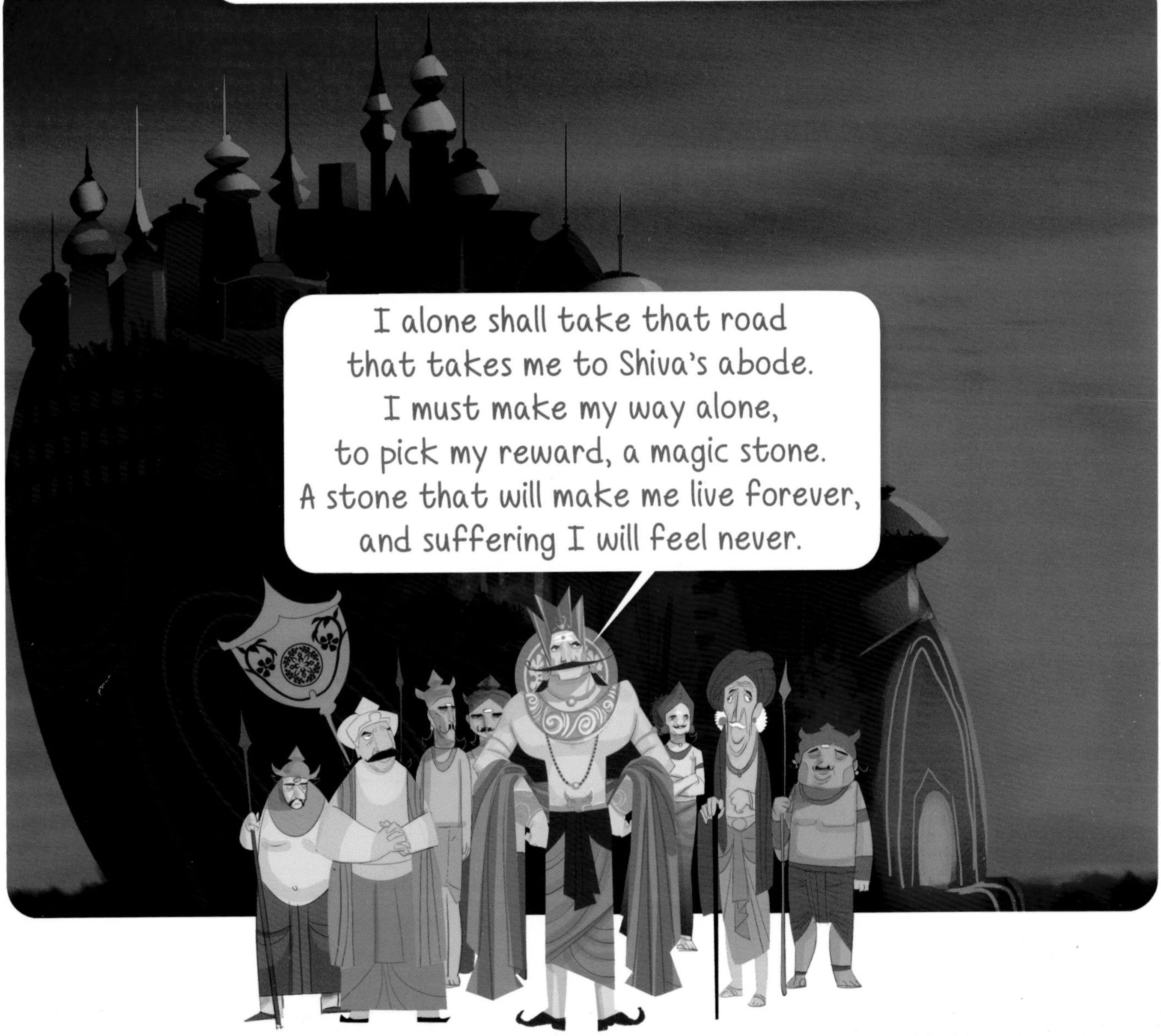
I alone shall take that road
that takes me to Shiva's abode.
I must make my way alone,
to pick my reward, a magic stone.
A stone that will make me live forever,
and suffering I will feel never.

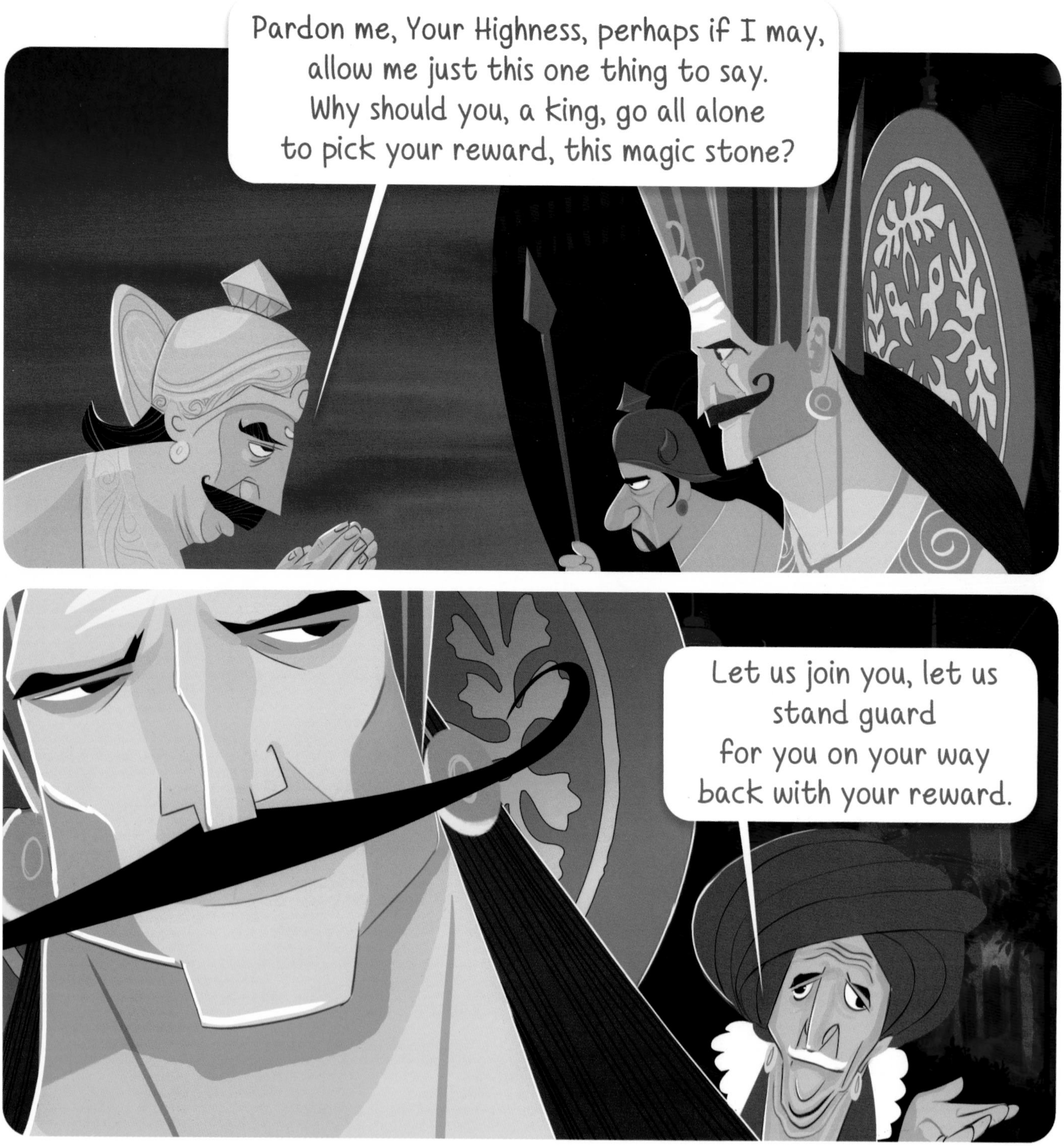
Pardon me, Your Highness, perhaps if I may, allow me just this one thing to say. Why should you, a king, go all alone to pick your reward, this magic stone?
Let us join you, let us stand guard for you on your way back with your reward.

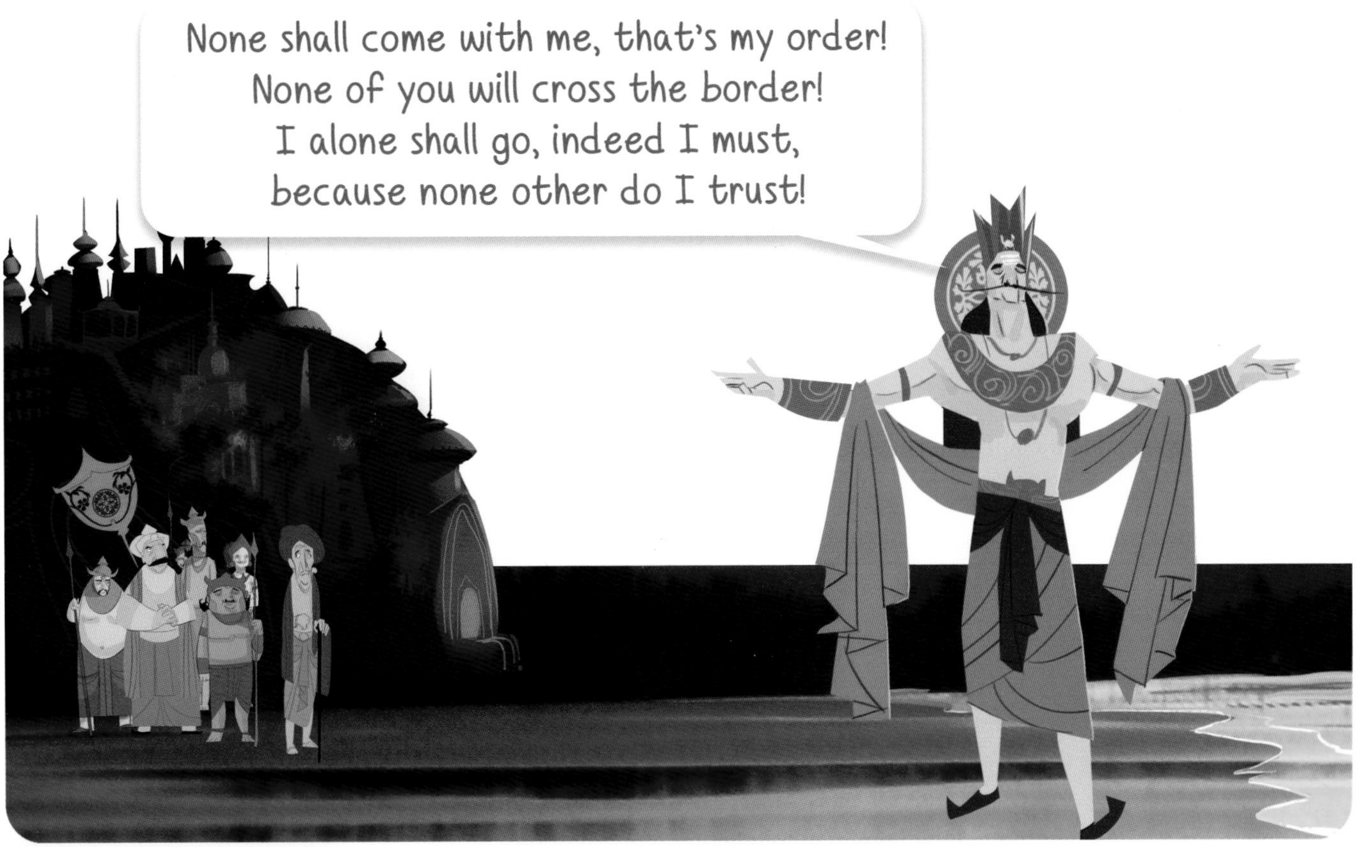
None shall come with me, that's my order!
None of you will cross the border!
I alone shall go, indeed I must,
because none other do I trust!

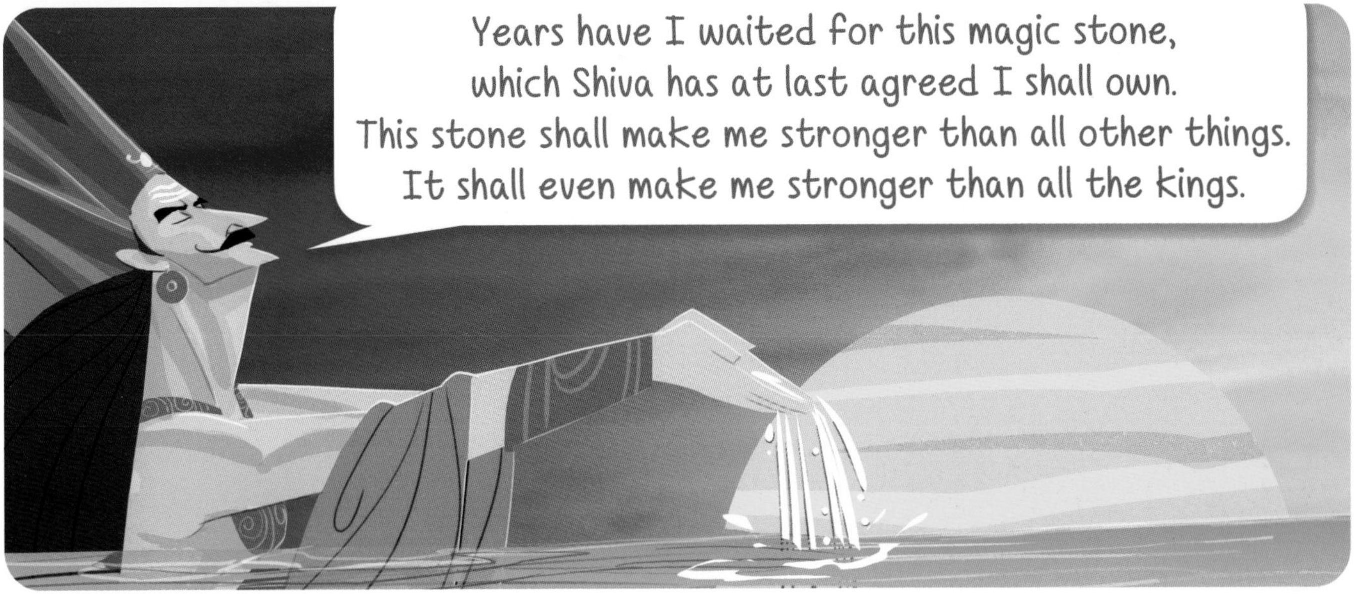
Years have I waited for this magic stone,
which Shiva has at last agreed I shall own.
This stone shall make me stronger than all other things.
It shall even make me stronger than all the kings.

Meanwhile, very, very, far away,
little Ganesha is busy at play.

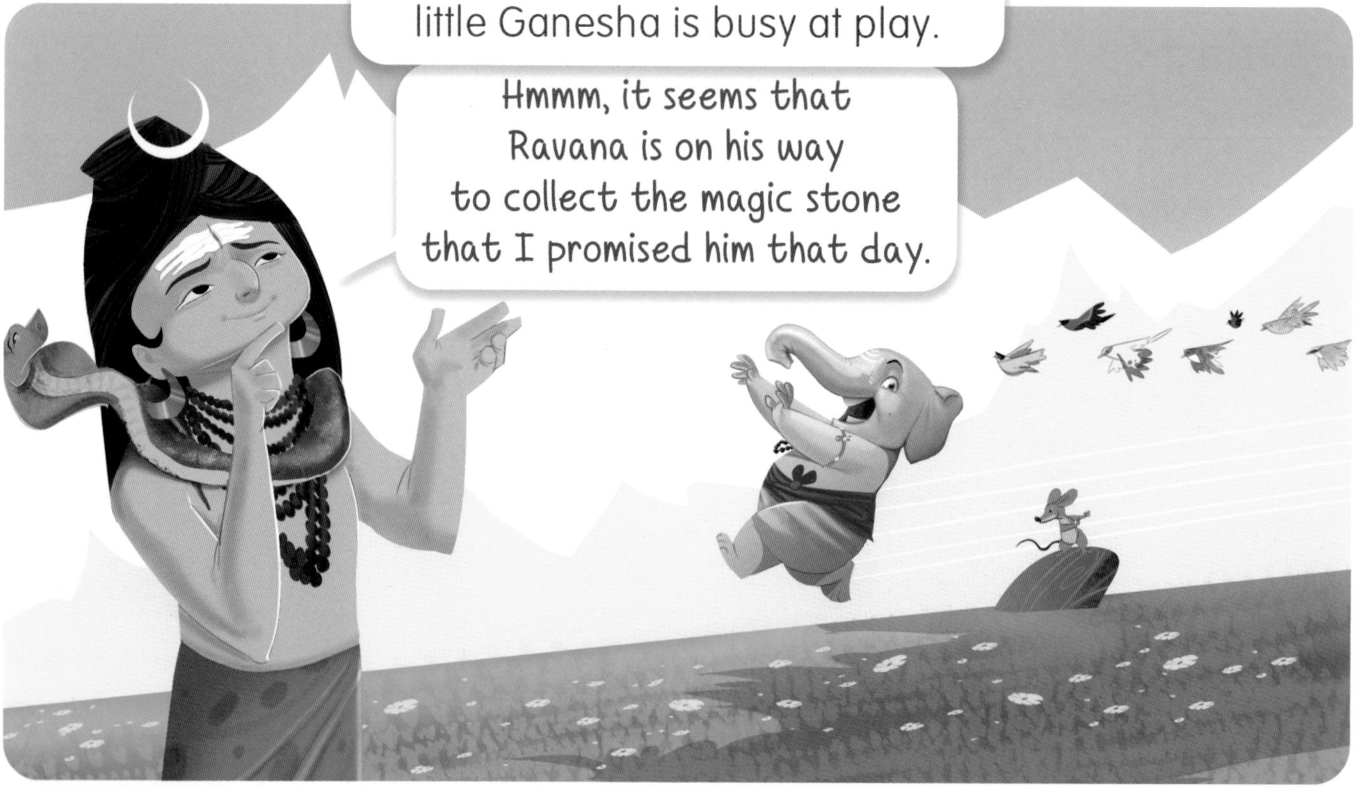
Hmmm, it seems that Ravana is on his way to collect the magic stone that I promised him that day.

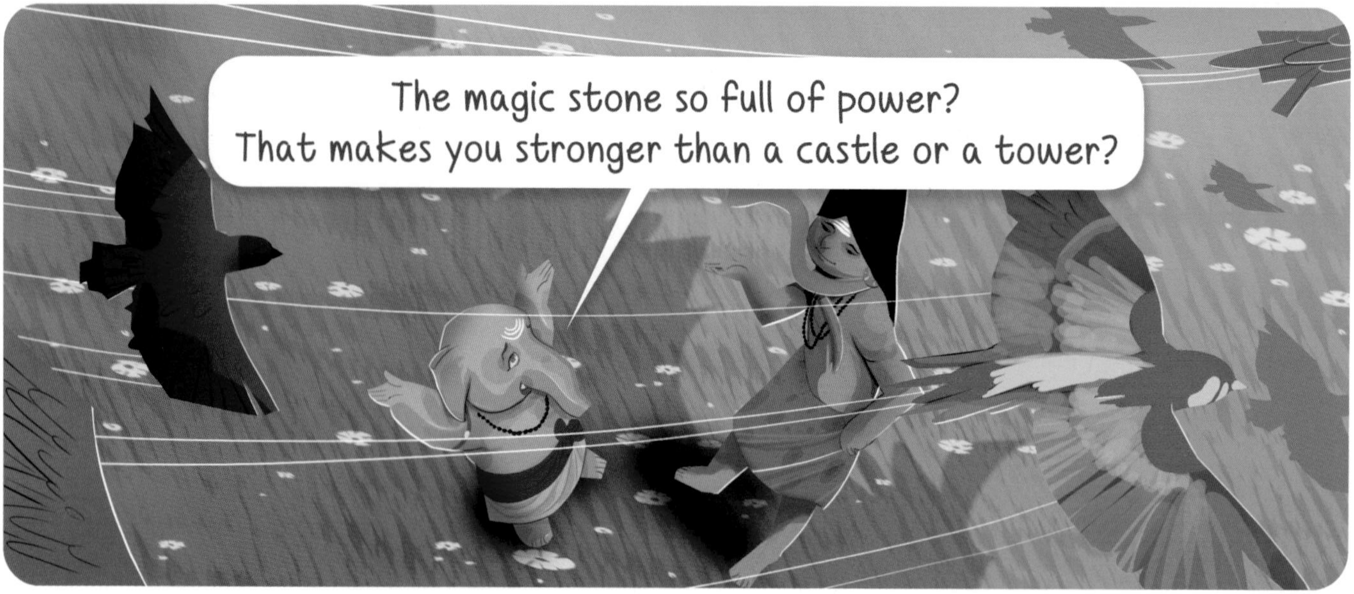
The magic stone so full of power? That makes you stronger than a castle or a tower?

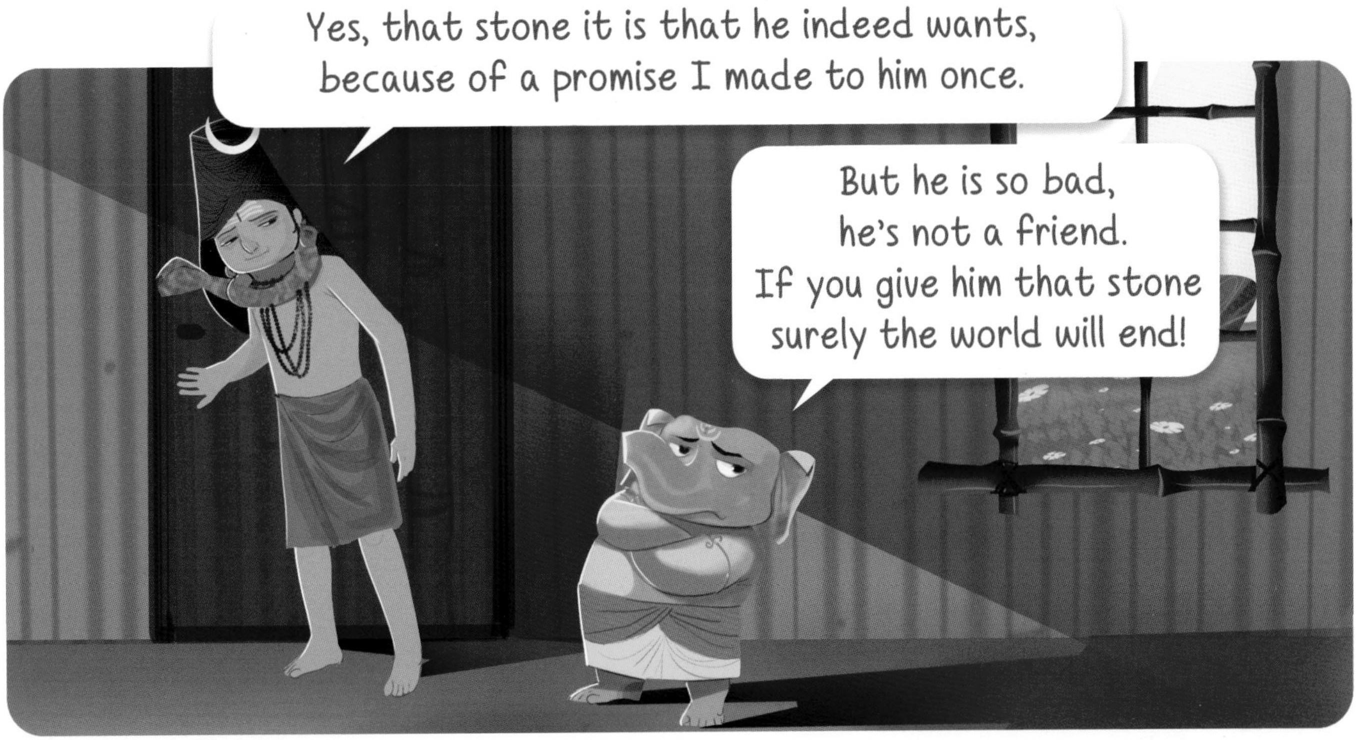
Yes, that stone it is that he indeed wants, because of a promise I made to him once.
But he is so bad, he's not a friend. If you give him that stone surely the world will end!

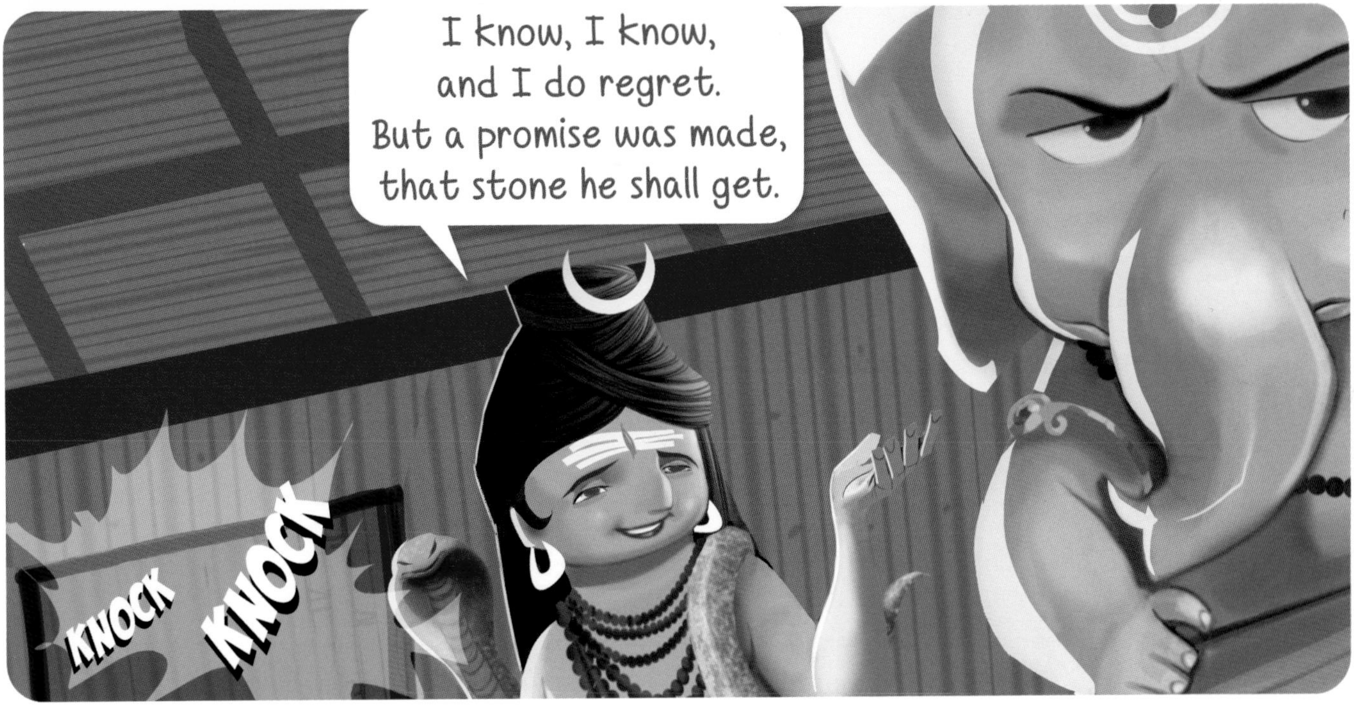
I know, I know, and I do regret. But a promise was made, that stone he shall get.
KNOCK
KNOCK

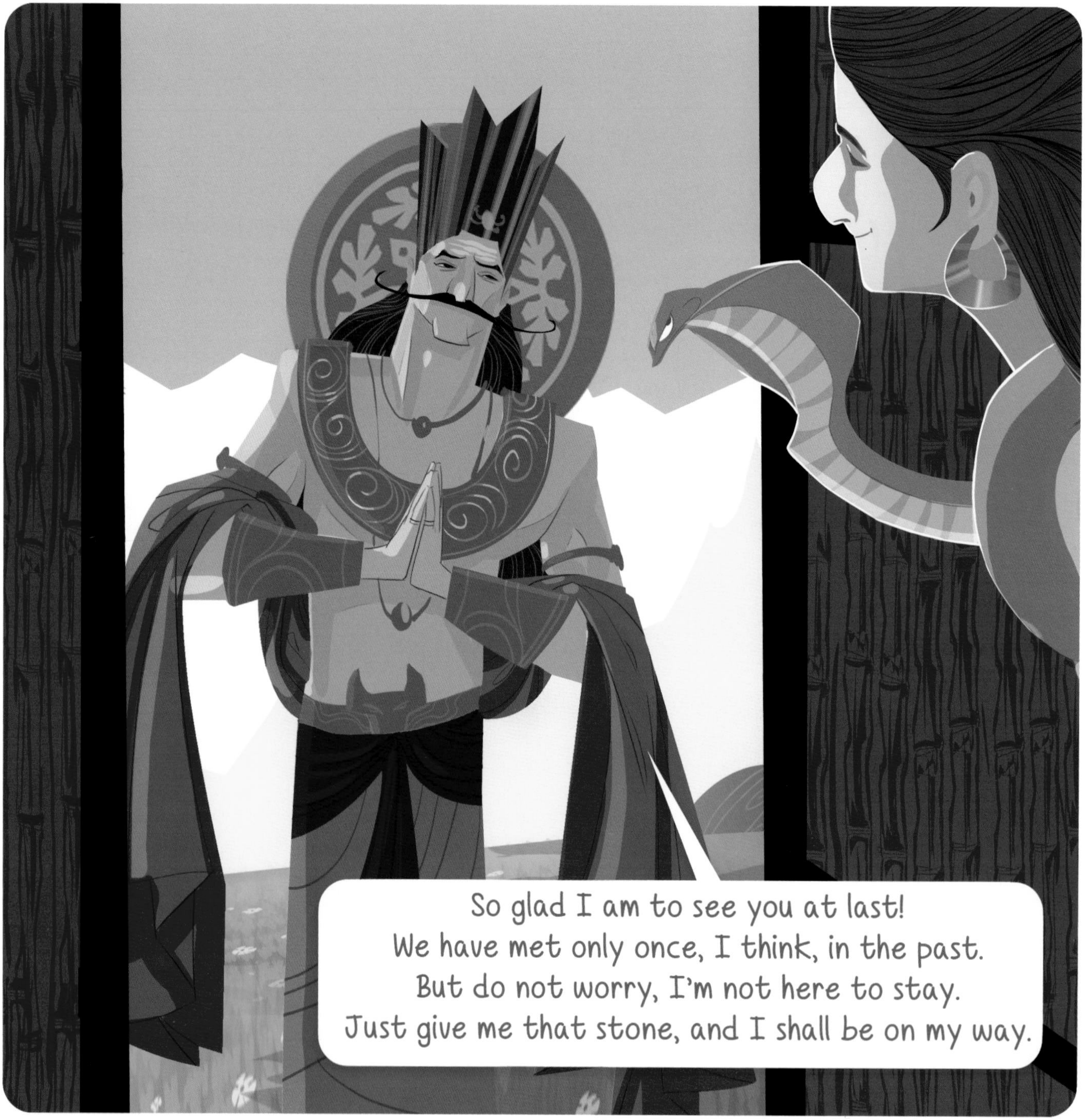
So glad I am to see you at last!
We have met only once, I think, in the past.
But do not worry, I'm not here to stay.
Just give me that stone, and I shall be on my way.

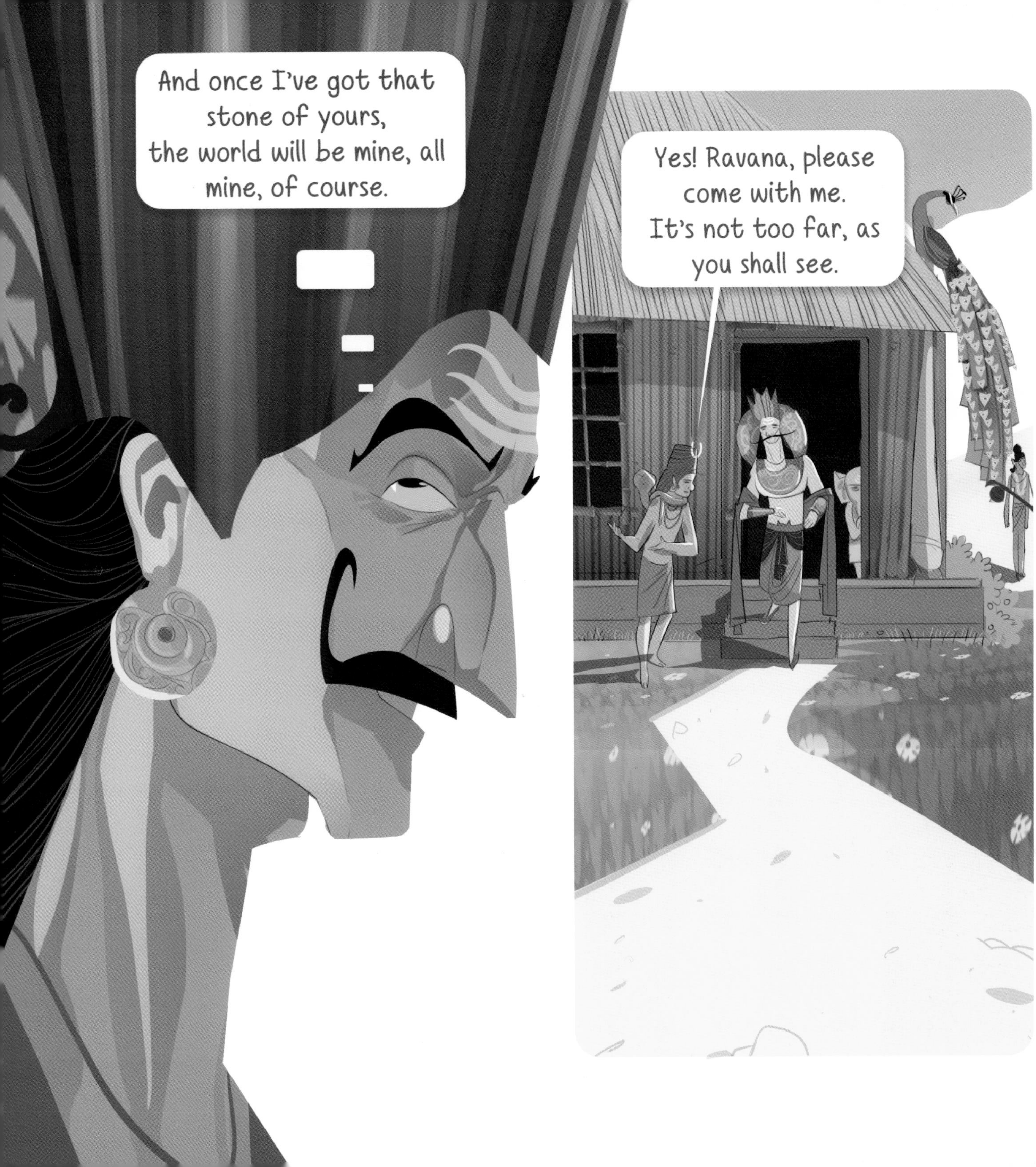
And once I've got that stone of yours, the world will be mine, all mine, of course.
Yes! Ravana, please come with me. It's not too far, as you shall see.

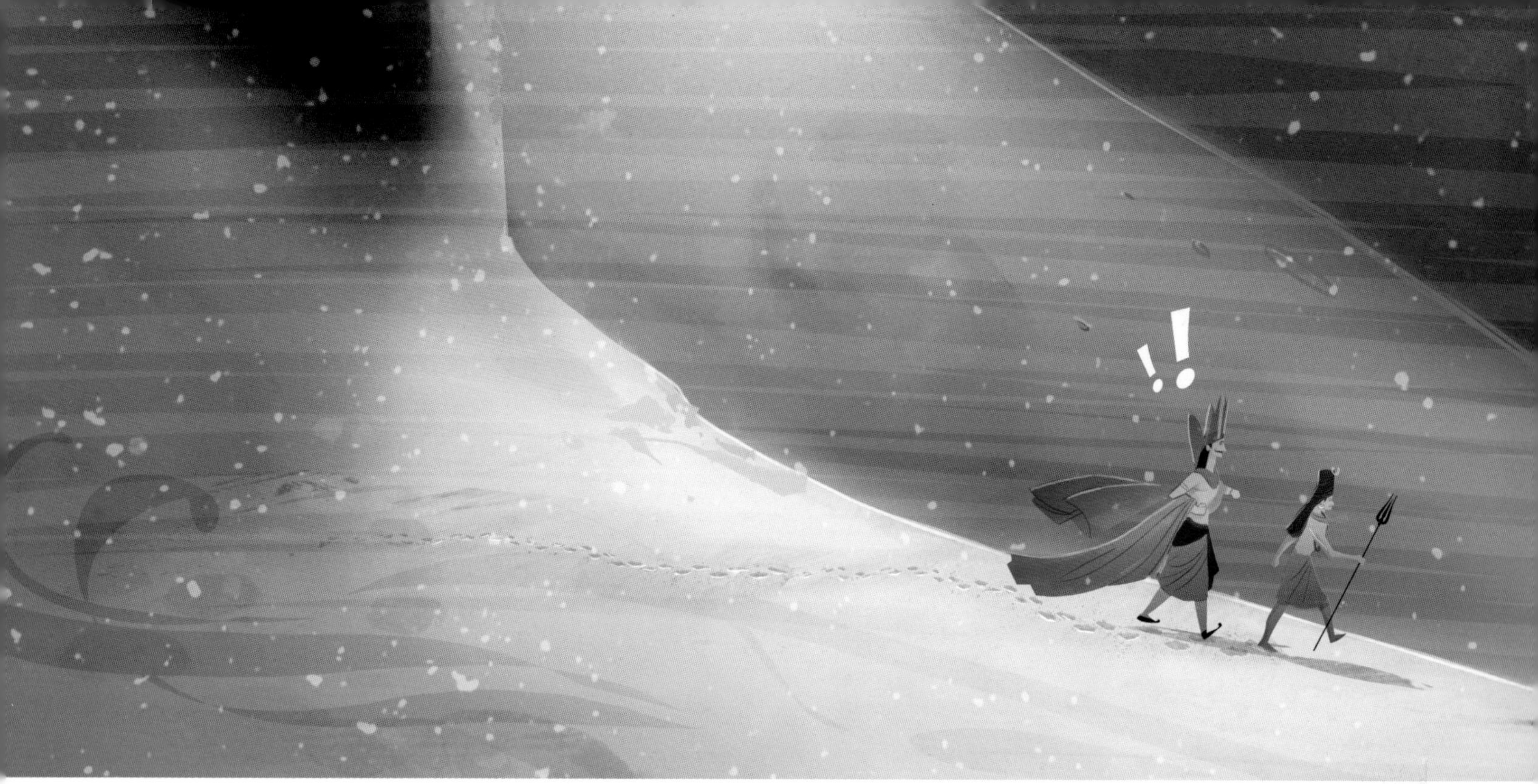

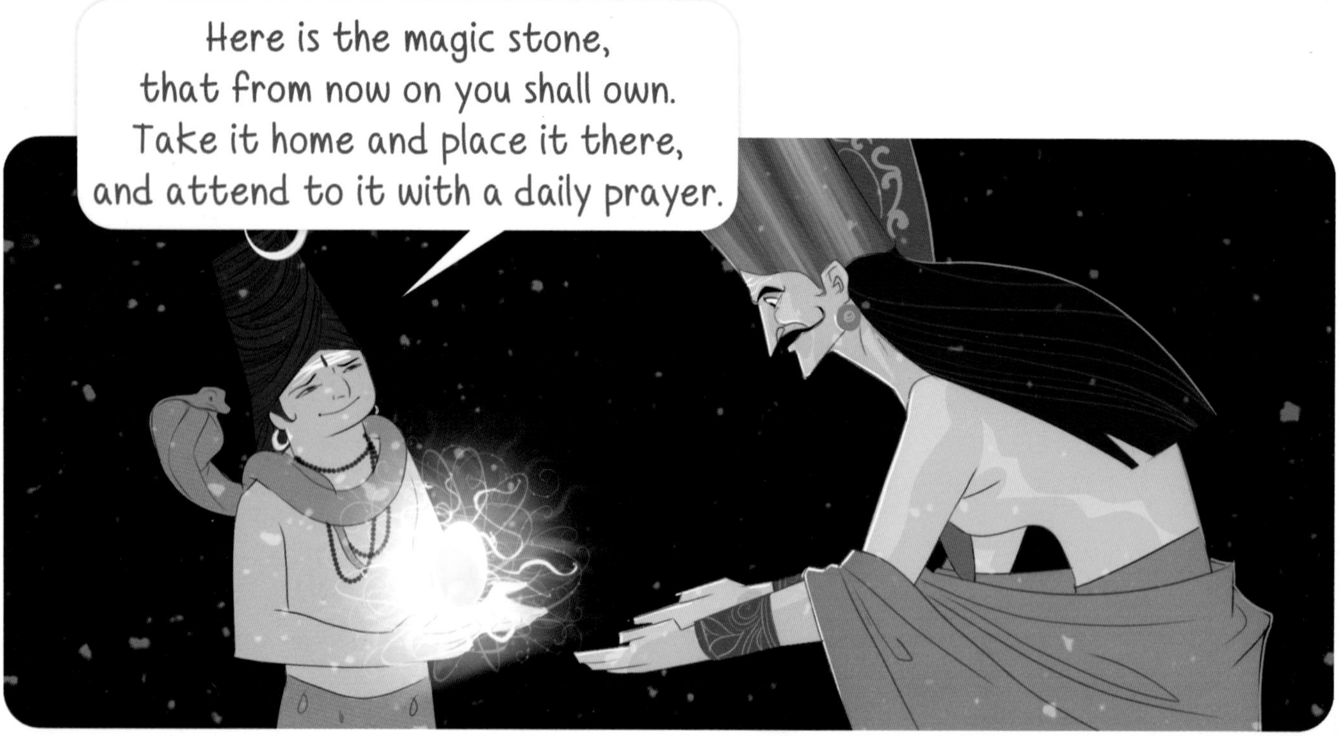
Here is the magic stone,
that from now on you shall own.
Take it home and place it there,
and attend to it with a daily prayer.

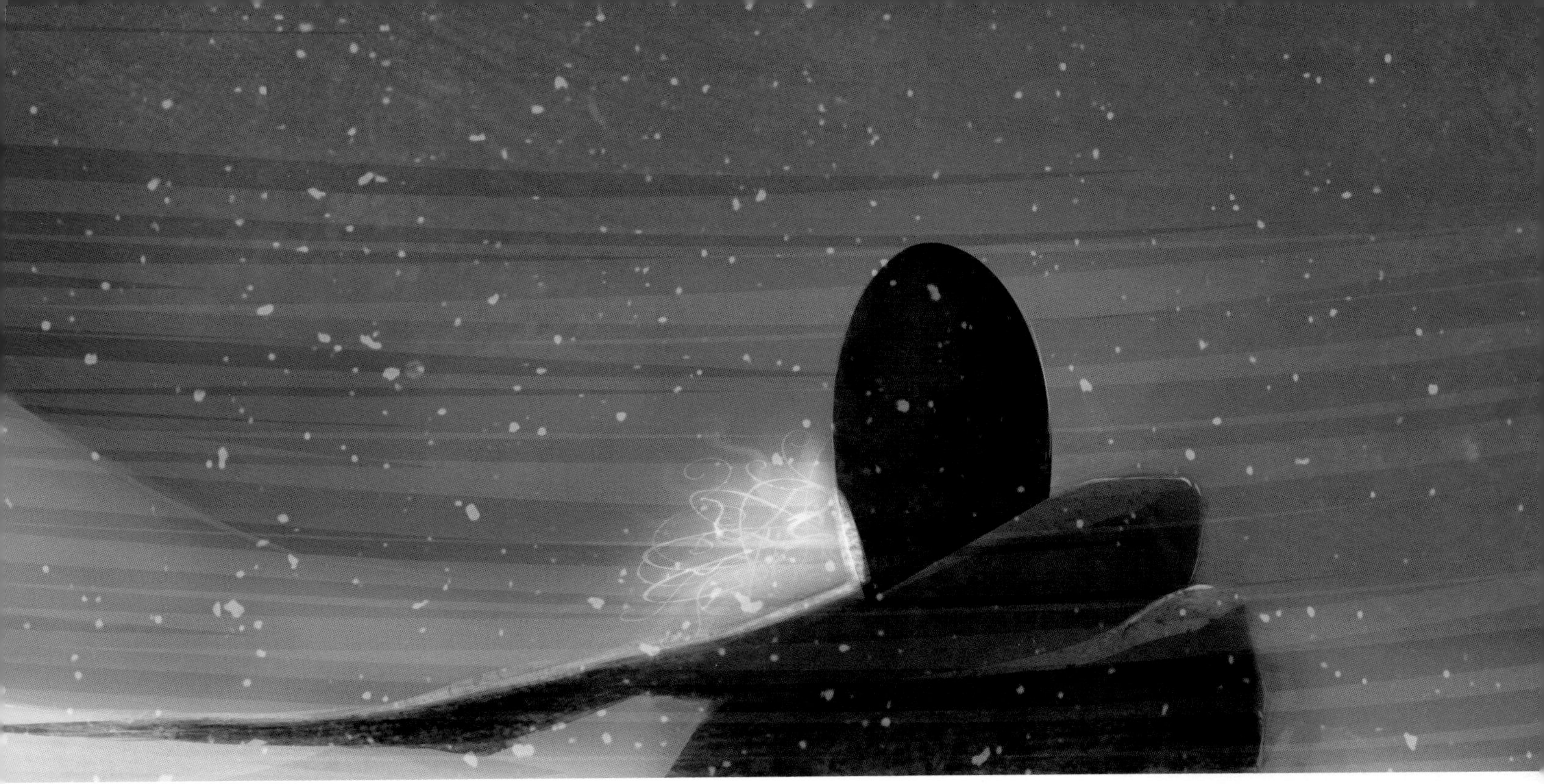

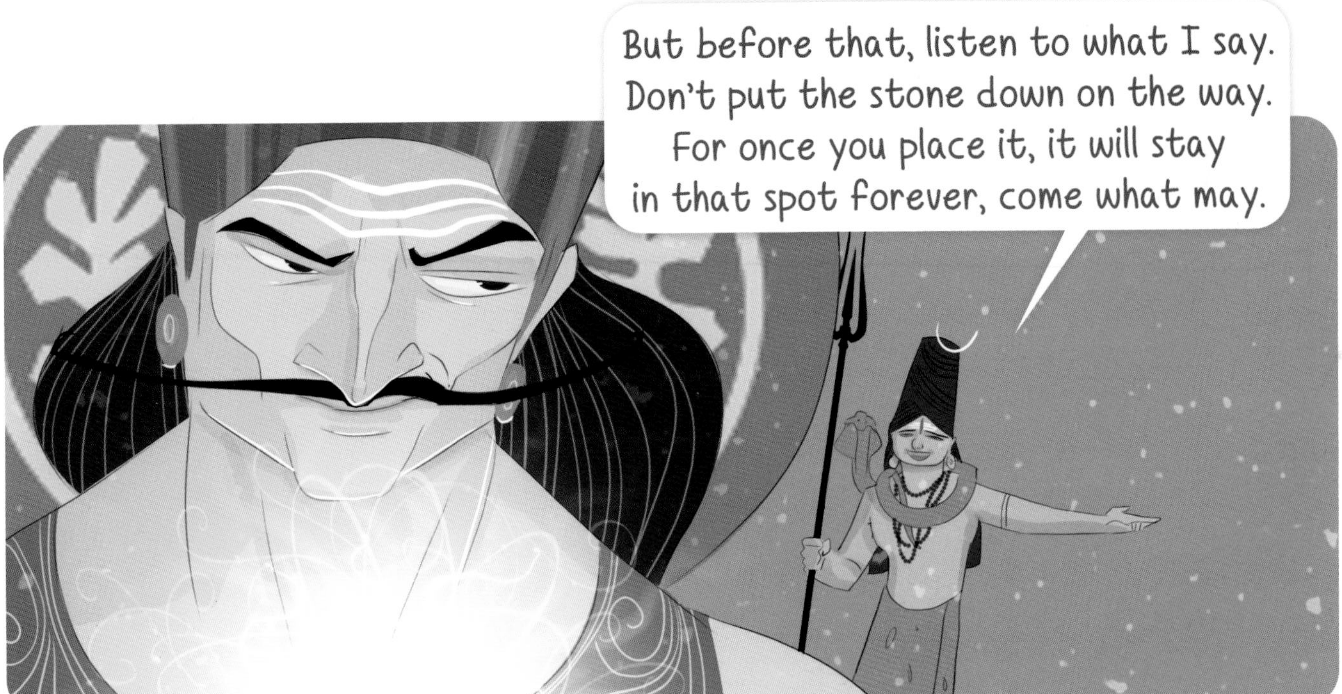
But before that, listen to what I say.
Don't put the stone down on the way.
For once you place it, it will stay
in that spot forever, come what may.

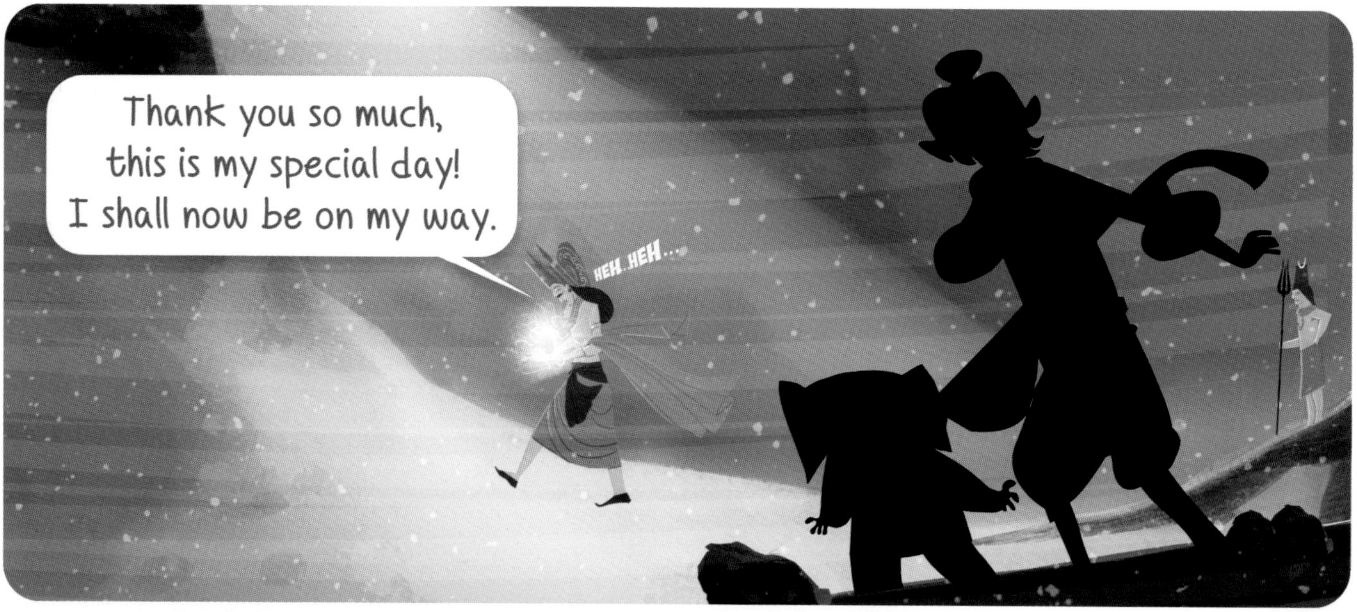
Thank you so much, this is my special day! I shall now be on my way.
HEH..HEH...

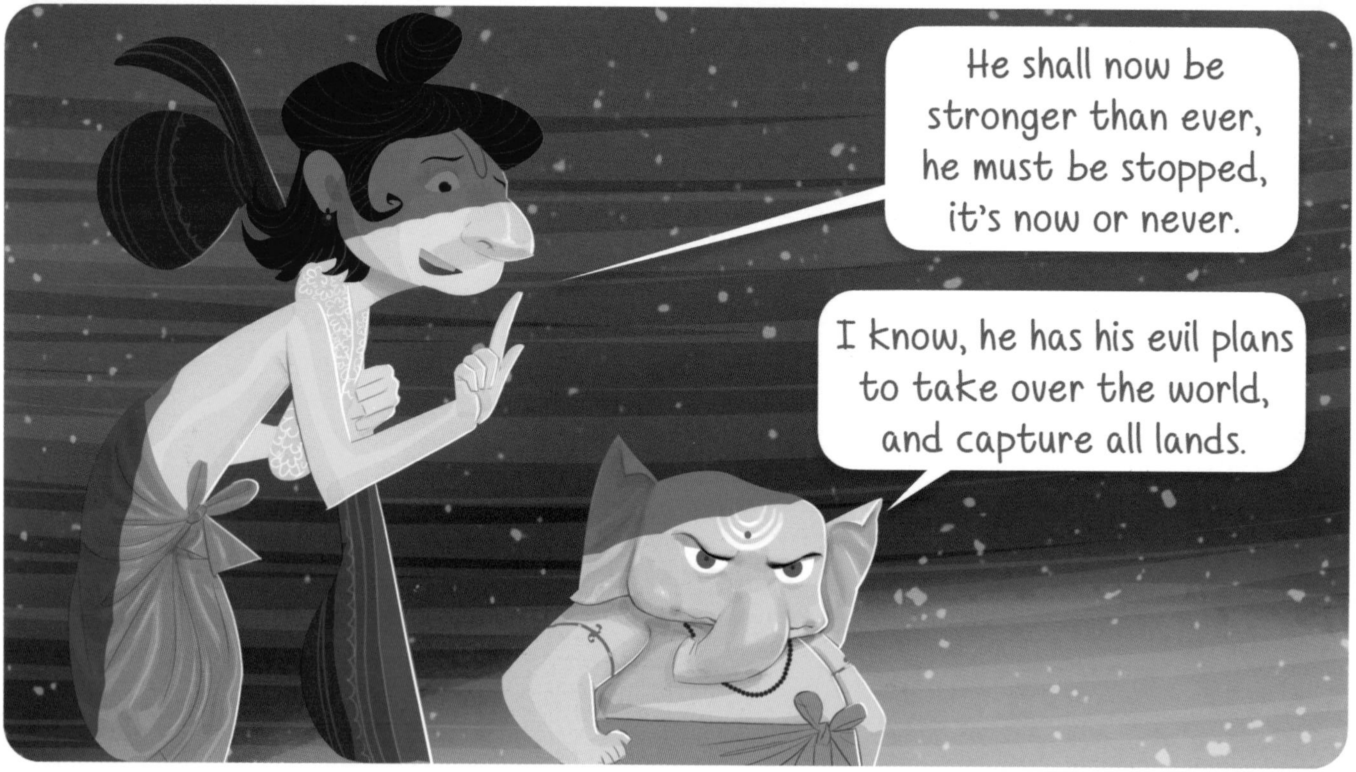
He shall now be stronger than ever, he must be stopped, it's now or never.
I know, he has his evil plans to take over the world, and capture all lands.

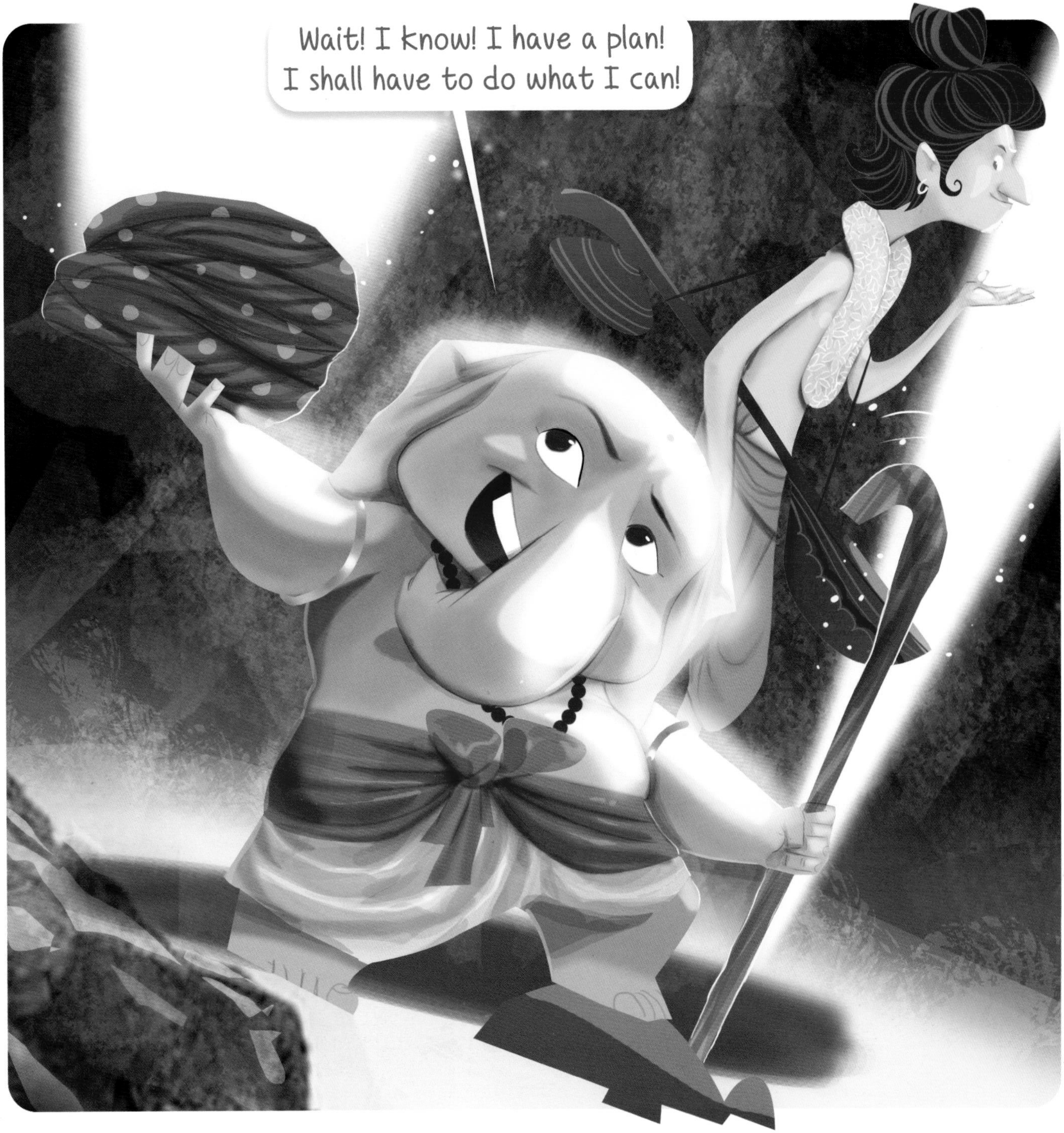
Wait! I know! I have a plan!
I shall have to do what I can!

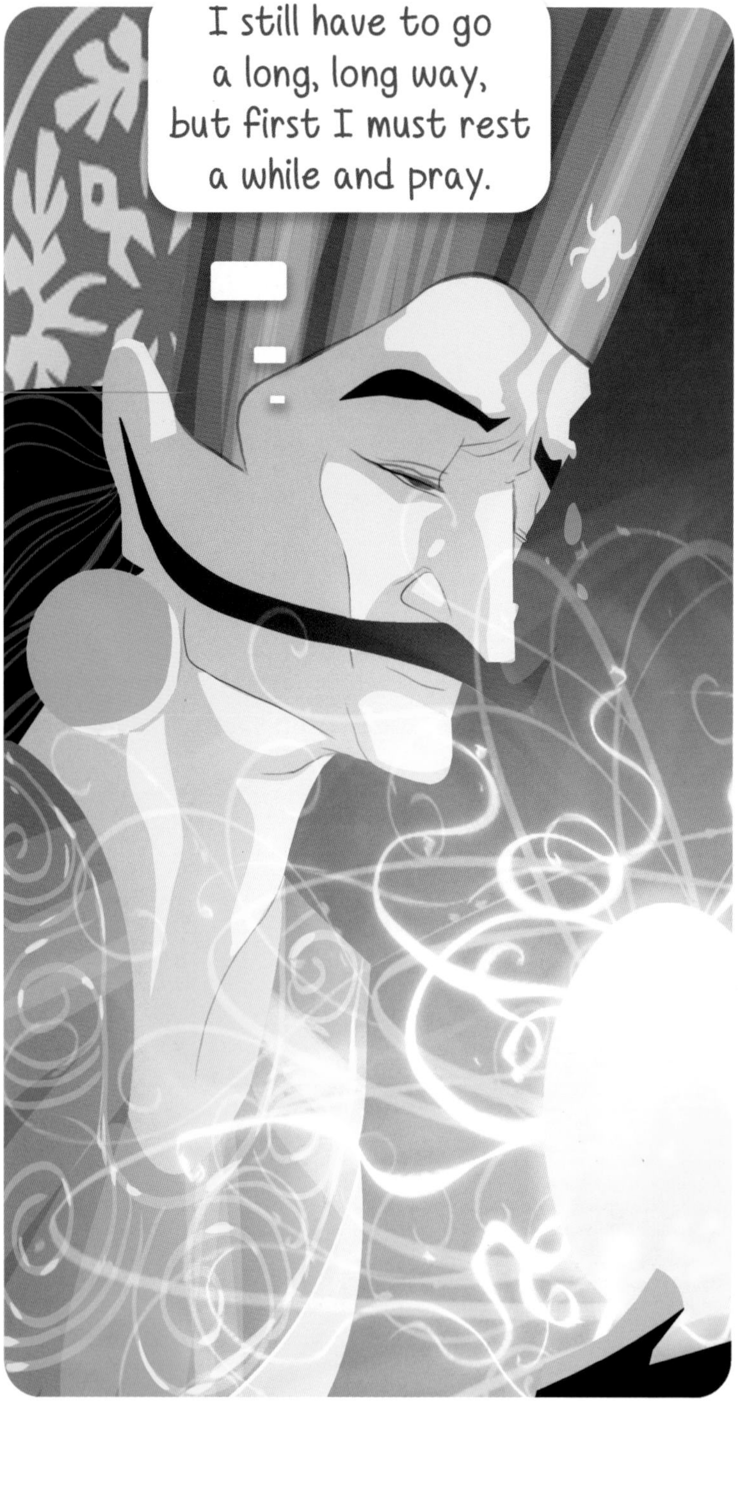
I still have to go
a long, long way,
but first I must rest
a while and pray.

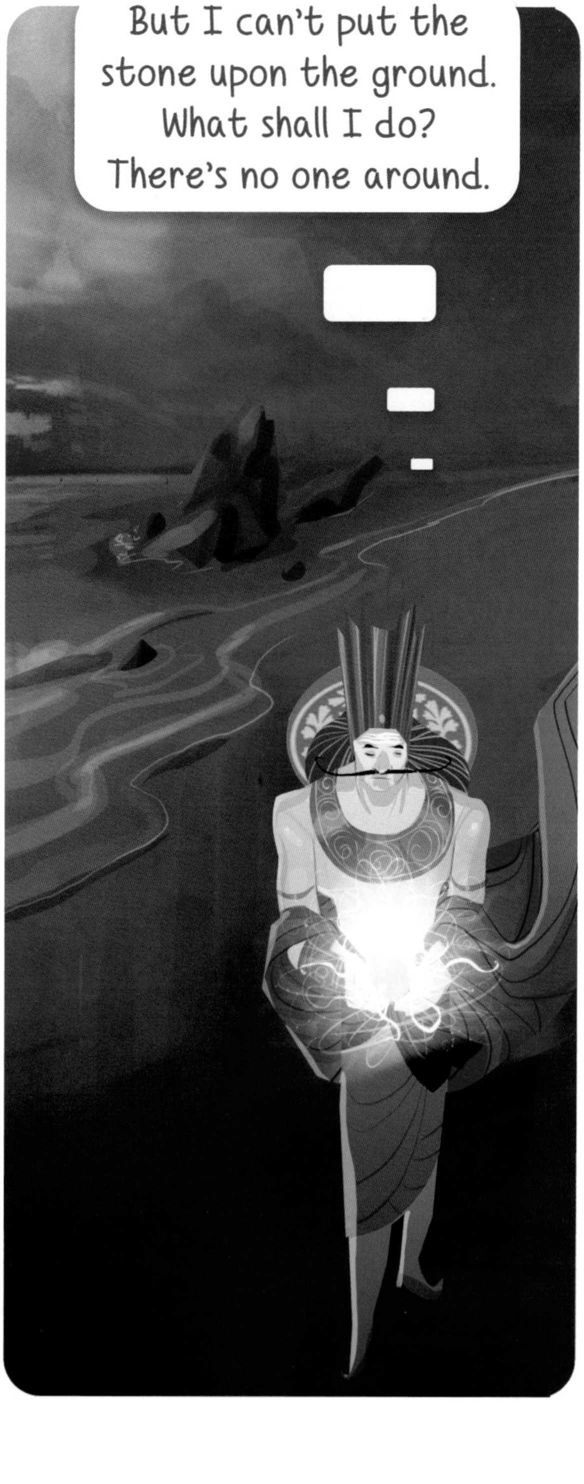
But I can't put the
stone upon the ground.
What shall I do?
There's no one around.

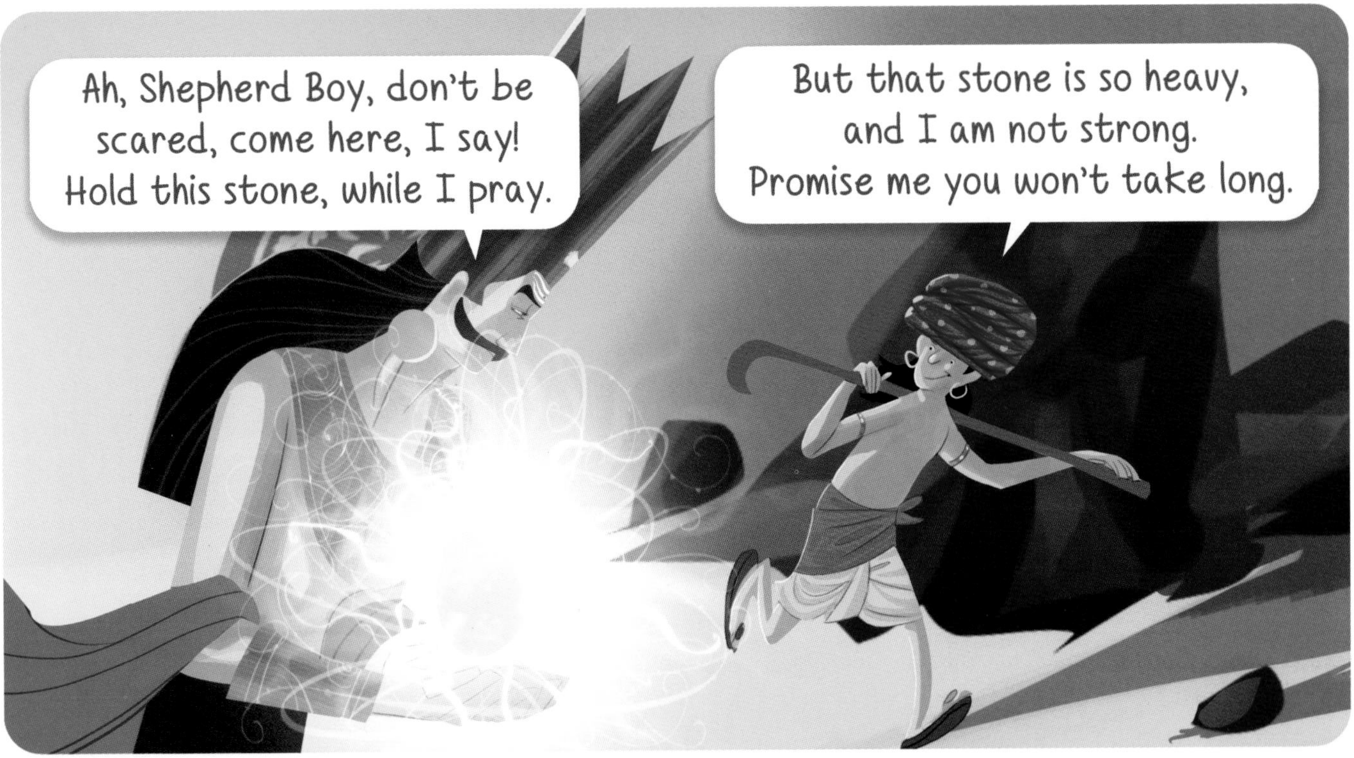
Ah, Shepherd Boy, don't be scared, come here, I say! Hold this stone, while I pray.
But that stone is so heavy, and I am not strong. Promise me you won't take long.

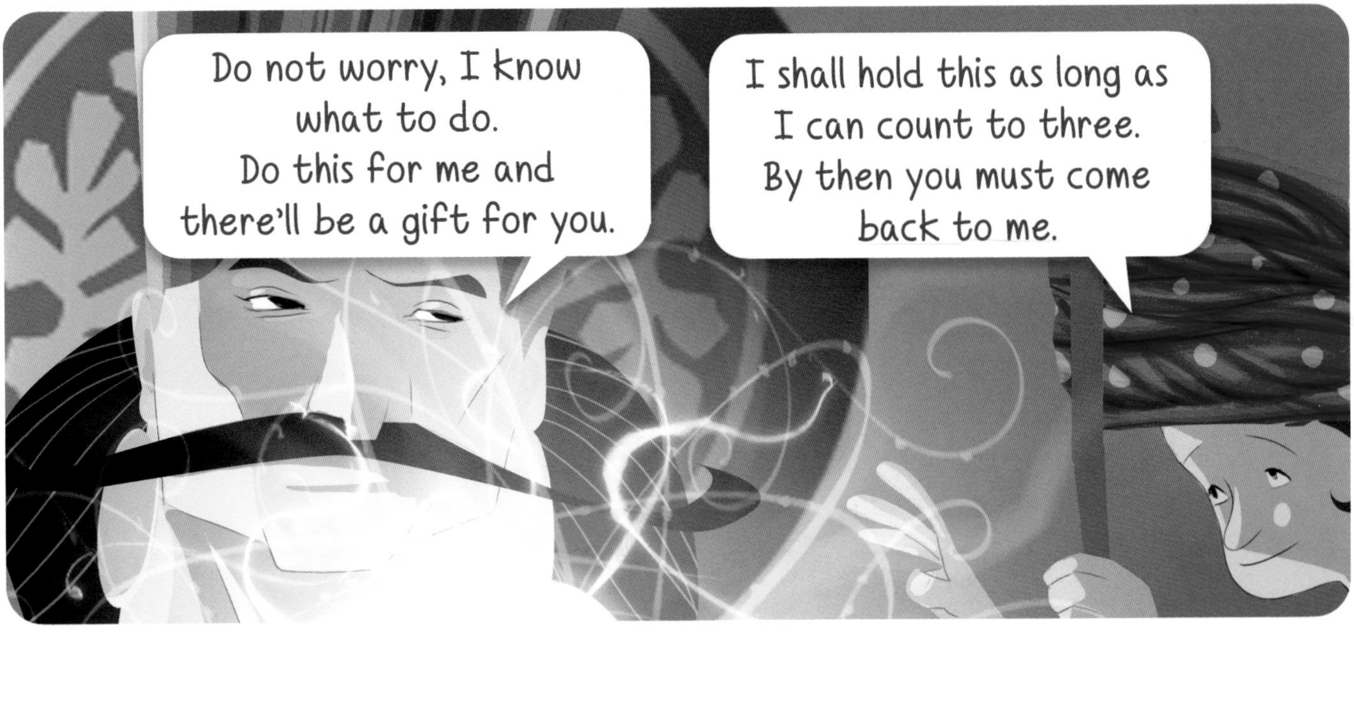
Do not worry, I know what to do. Do this for me and there'll be a gift for you.
I shall hold this as long as I can count to three. By then you must come back to me.

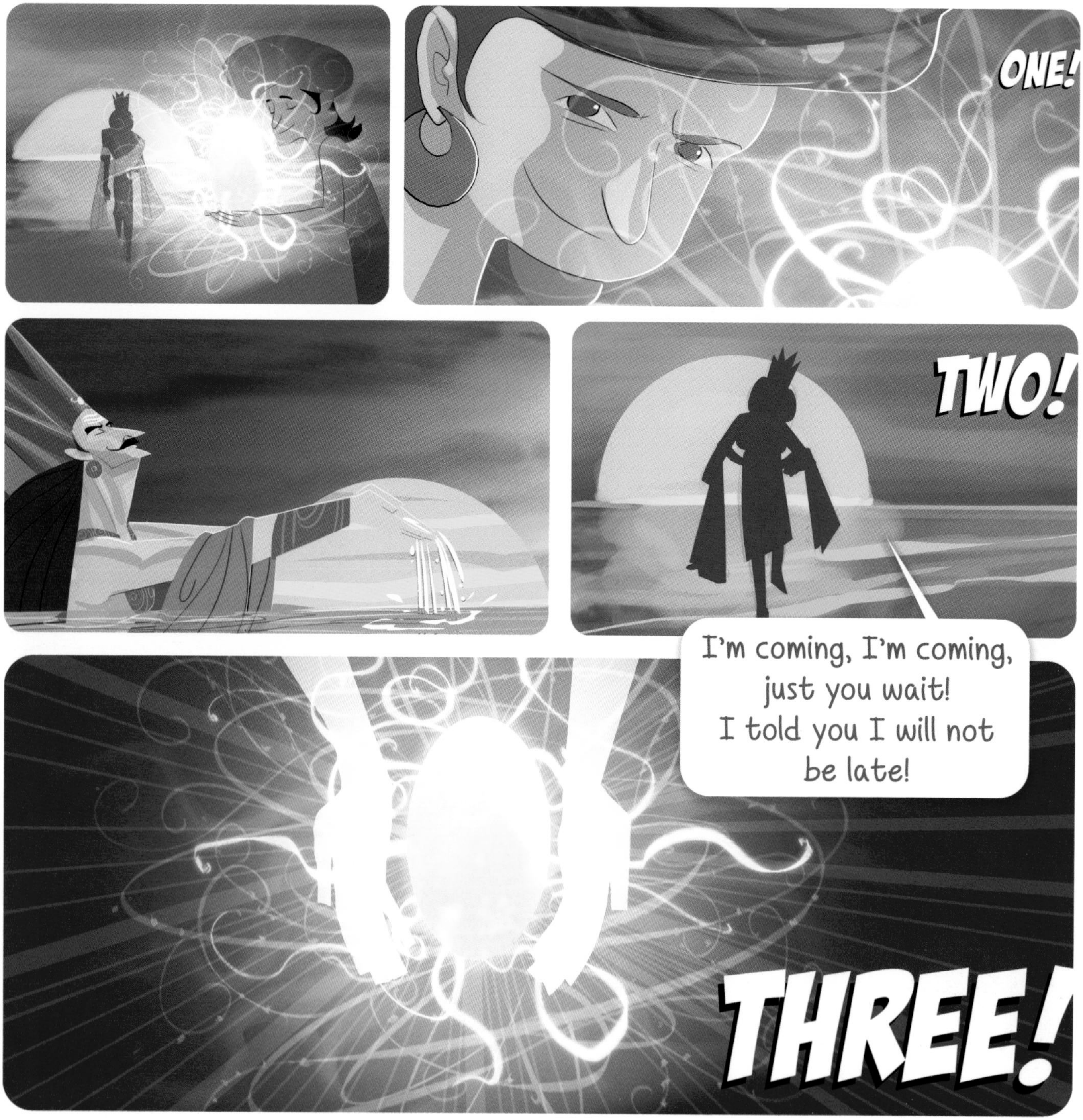
ONE!
TWO!
I'm coming, I'm coming, just you wait! I told you I will not be late!
THREE!

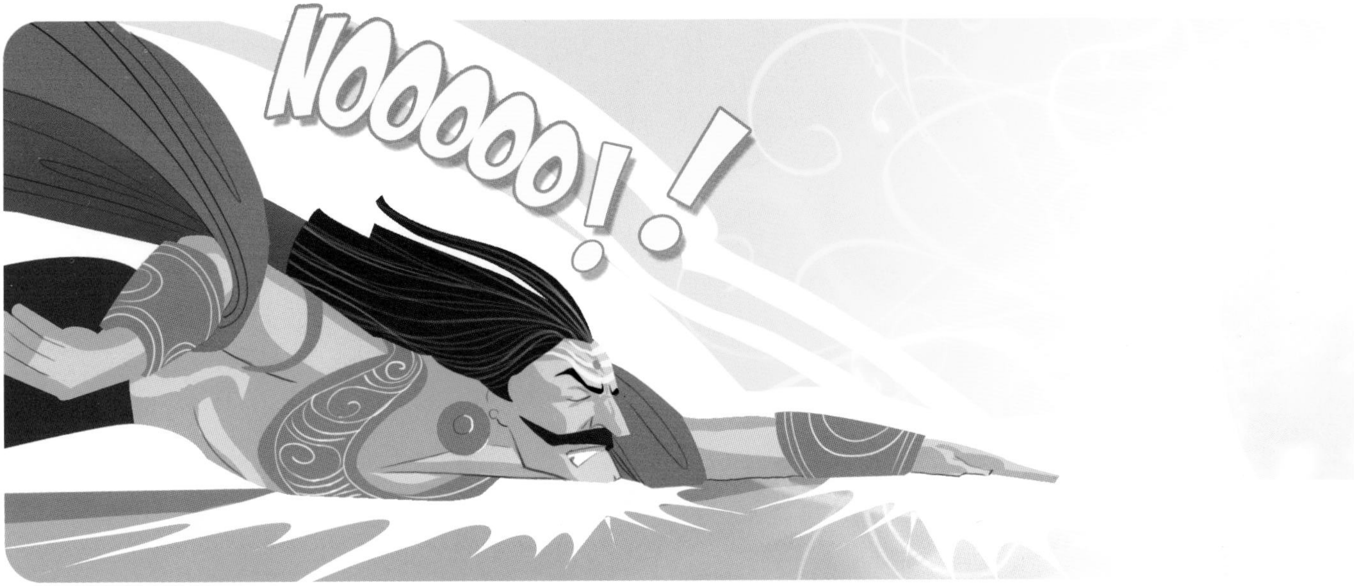
NOOOOOO!!

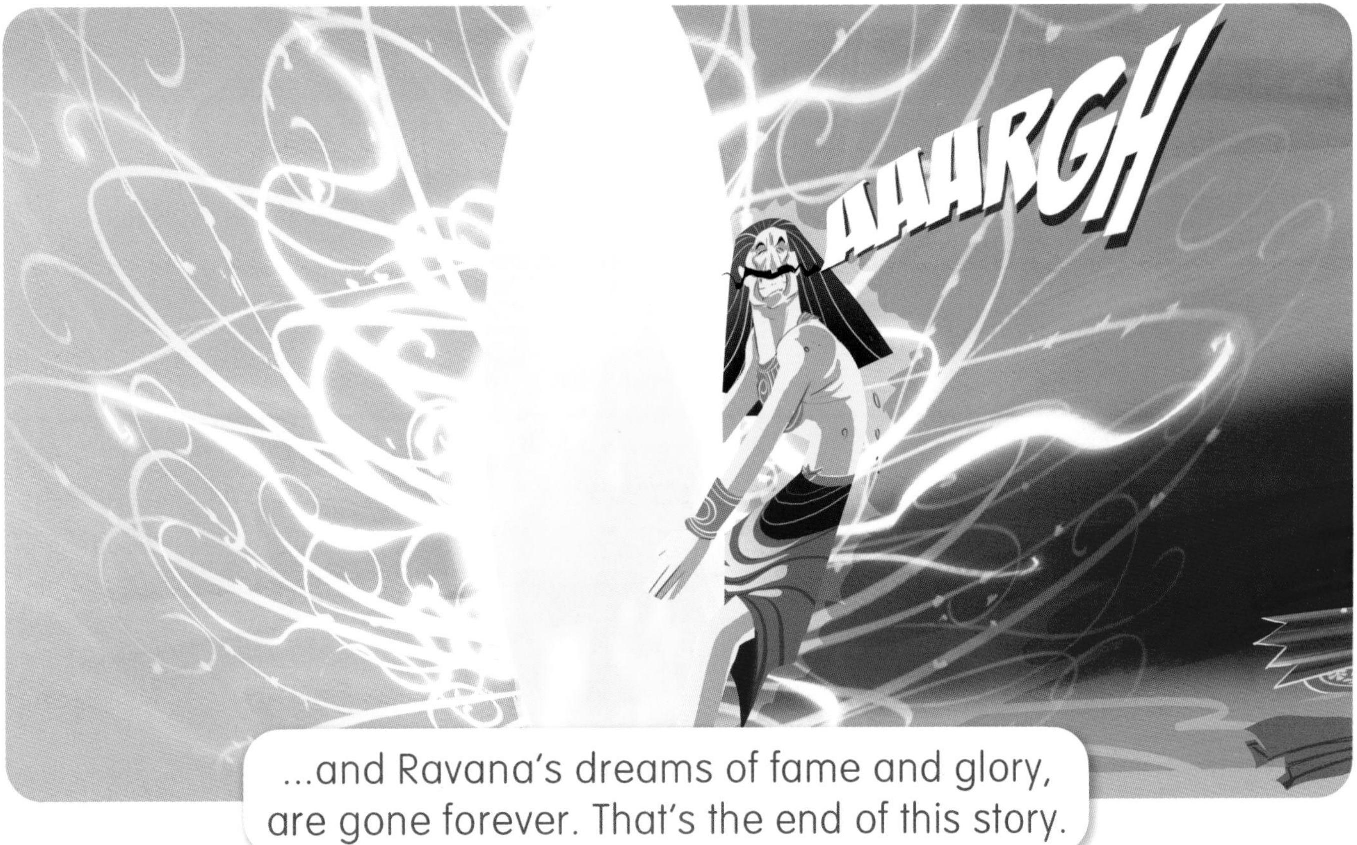
AAARGH
...and Ravana's dreams of fame and glory,
are gone forever. That's the end of this story.

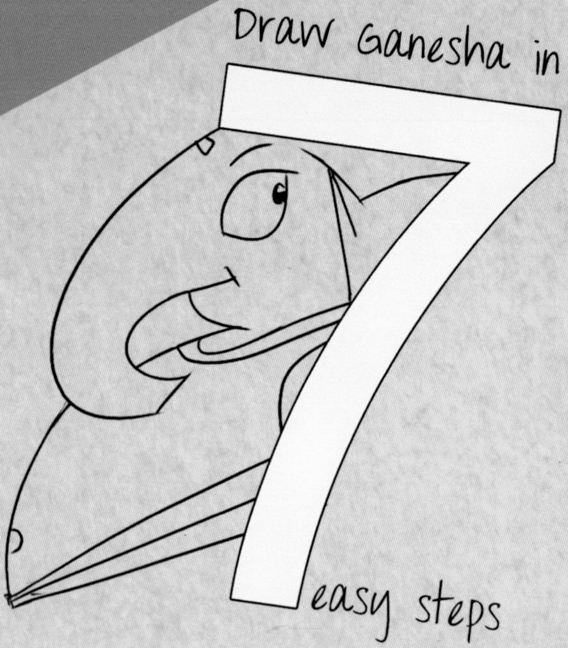
Draw Ganesha in
7
easy steps

1

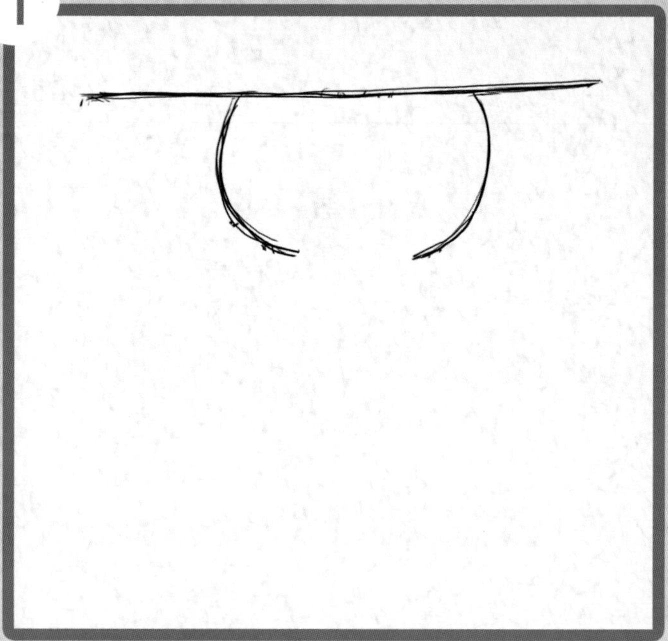

4

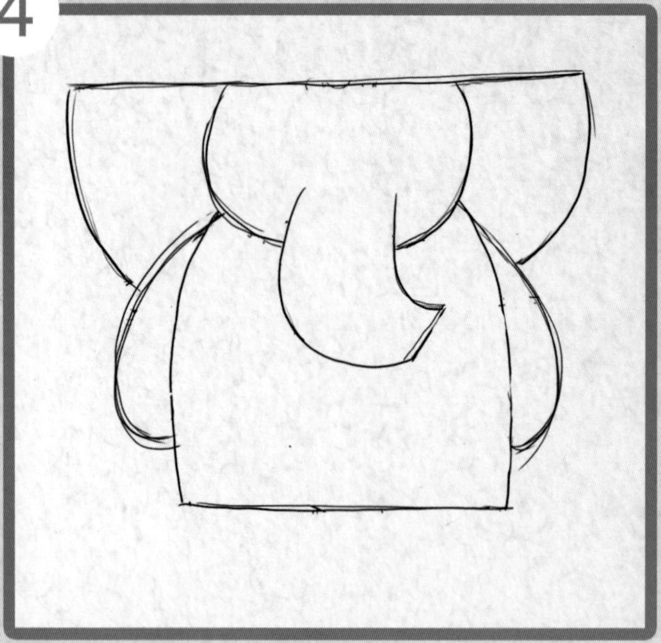

5

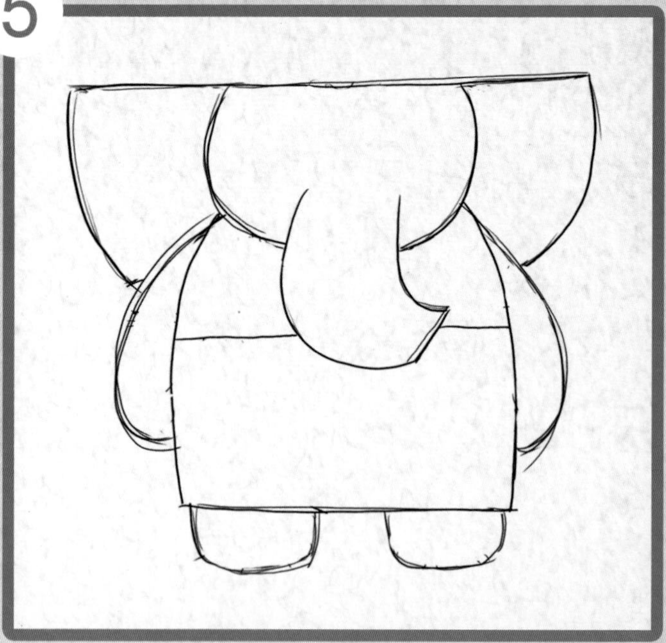

2

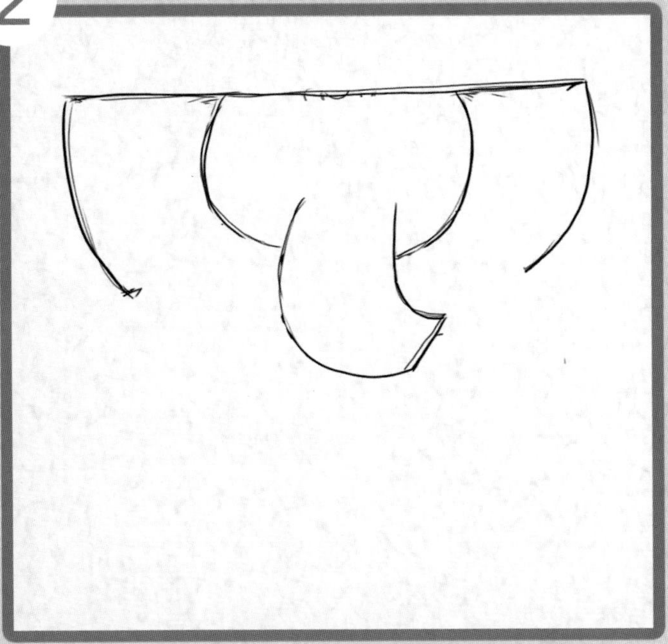

3

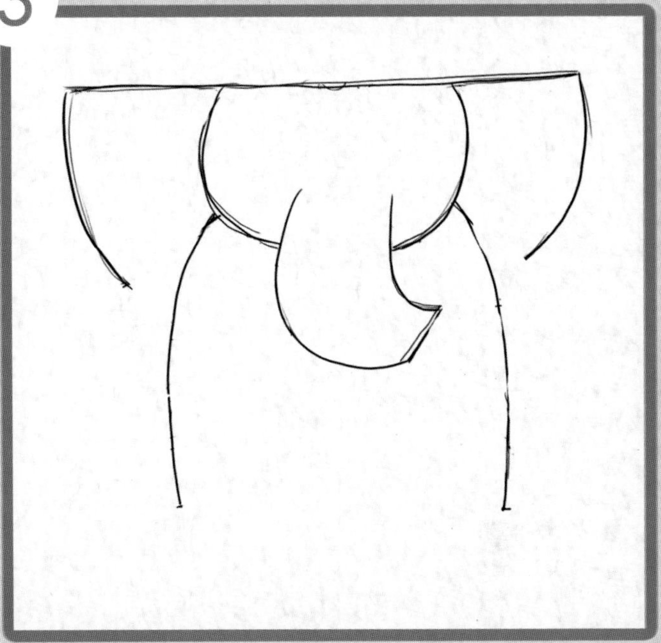

6

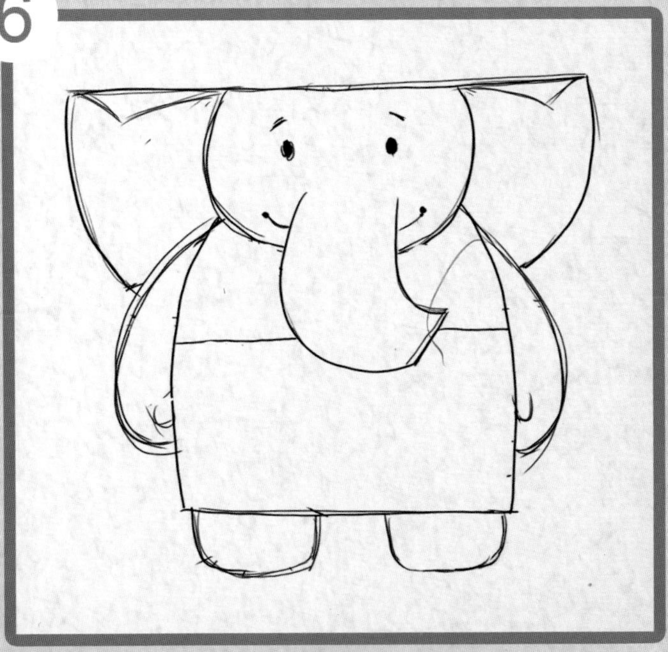

7

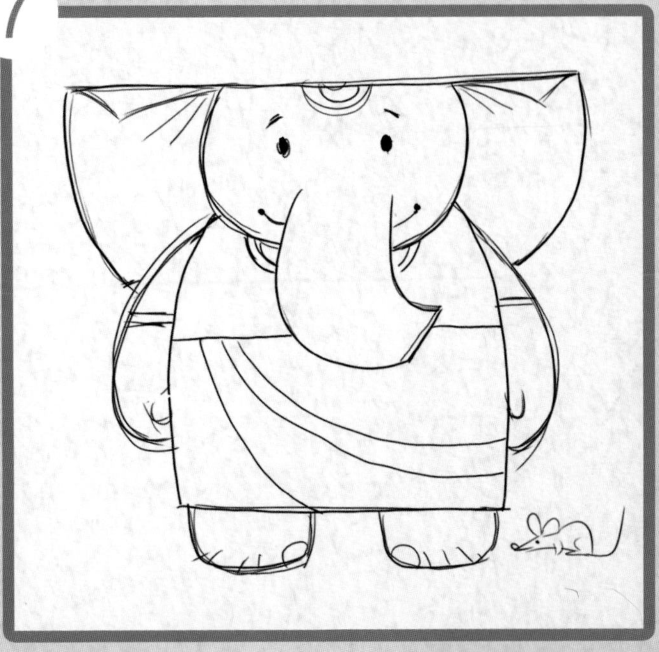

OTHER TITLES FROM CAMPFIRE JUNIOR

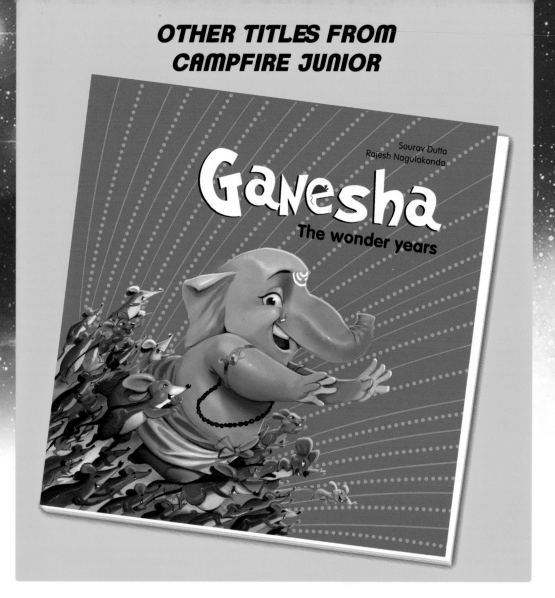

Sourav Dutta
Rajesh Nagulakonda

Ganesha
The wonder years

Little Ganesha is always getting up to mischief and this is your chance to join him and his family for two fun-filled adventures that will stay with you forever!

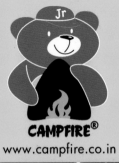

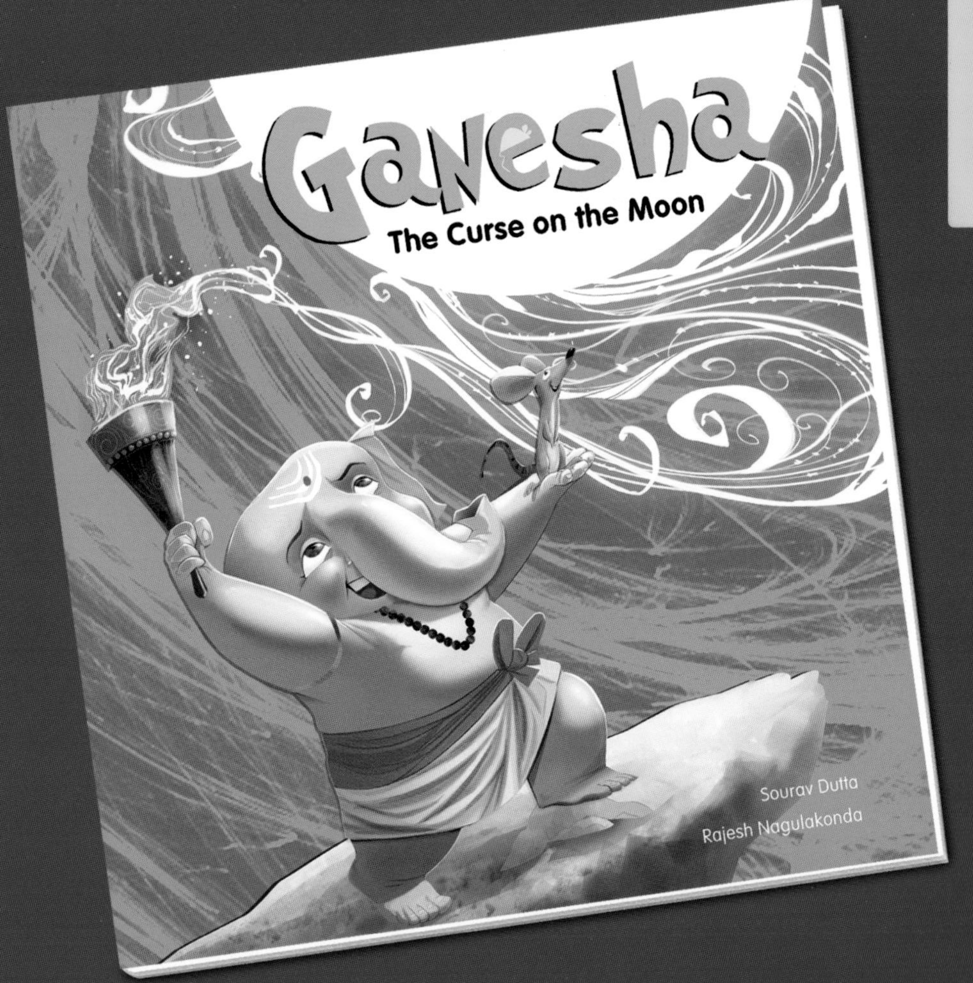
Ganesha
The Curse on the Moon
Sourav Dutta
Rajesh Nagulakonda

CAMPFIRE®
www.campfire.co.in

Why does sometimes the moon shine bright?
And why is it sometimes the darkest night?
What is it that causes the phases of the moon?
Read this book and you will find out soon.

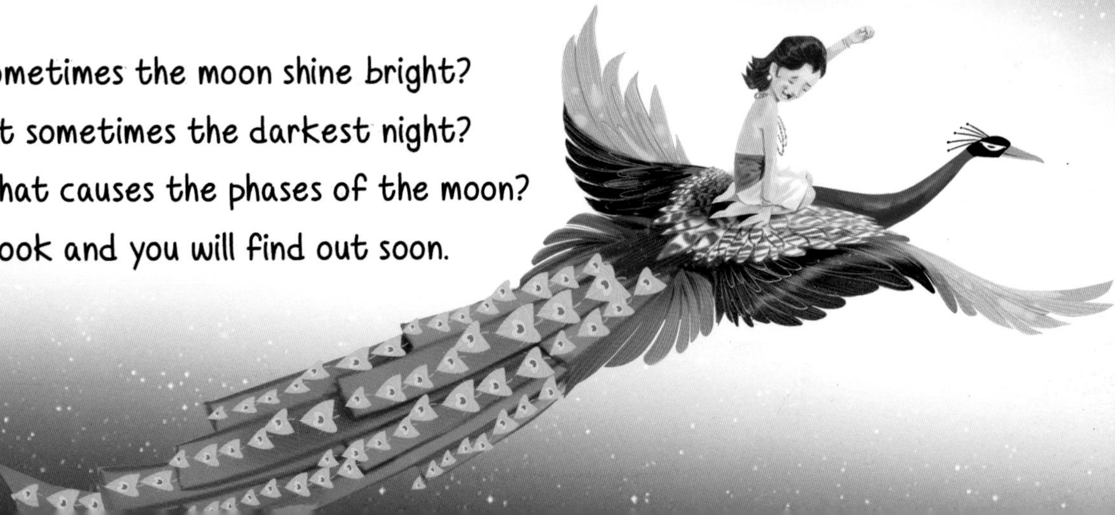

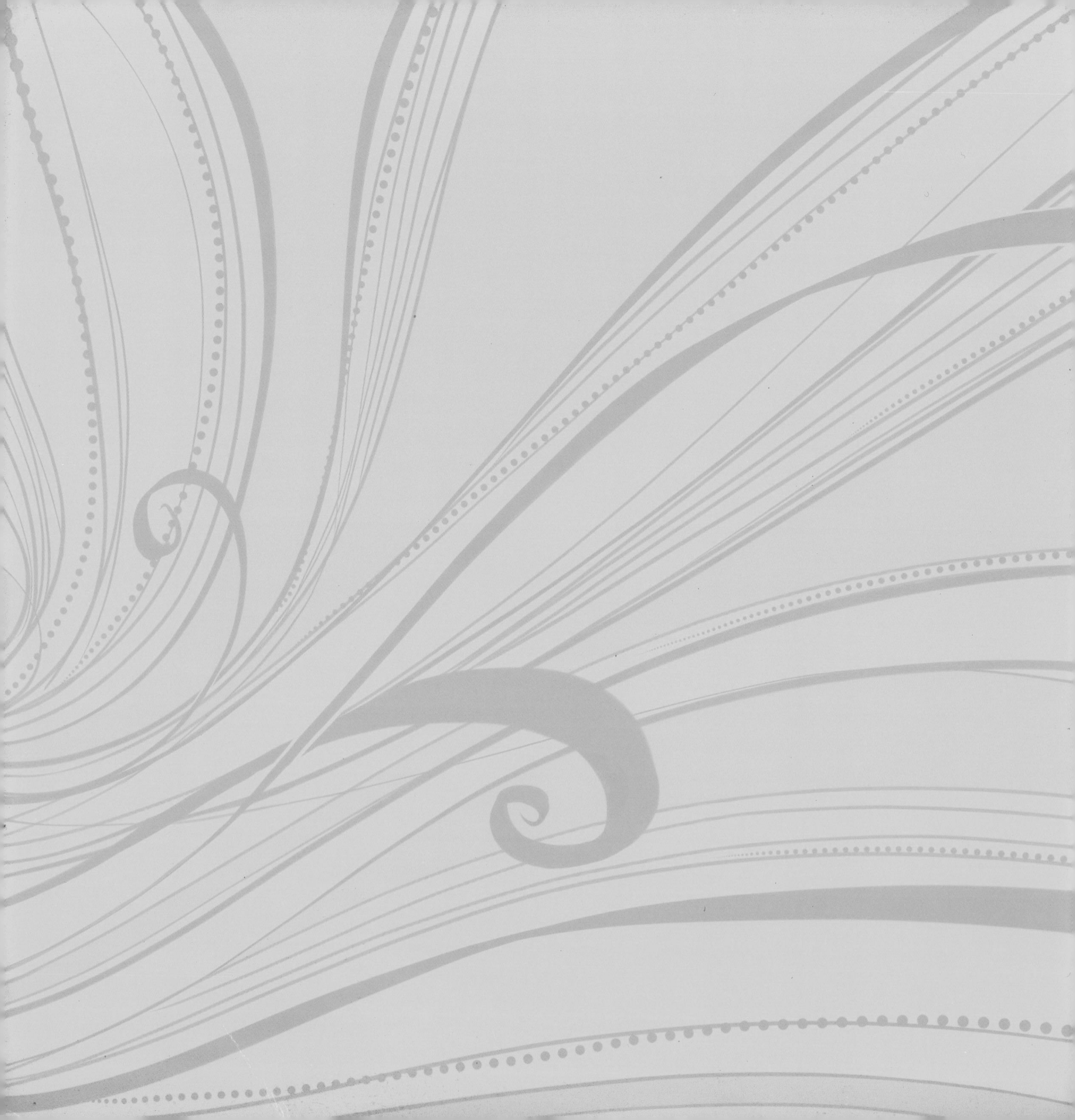